Story adaptation by
Rose Christopher

Illustrations by
Elizabeth Tate, Caroline LaVelle Egan, Studio IBOIX,
Michael Inman, Jean-Paul Orpiñas and
The Disney Storybook Artists

Design by Nadeem Zaidi

Printed in Melrose Park, Illinois, U.S.A.

Item #: 00006-962
SP20001459DEC2018
First Printing, December 2011

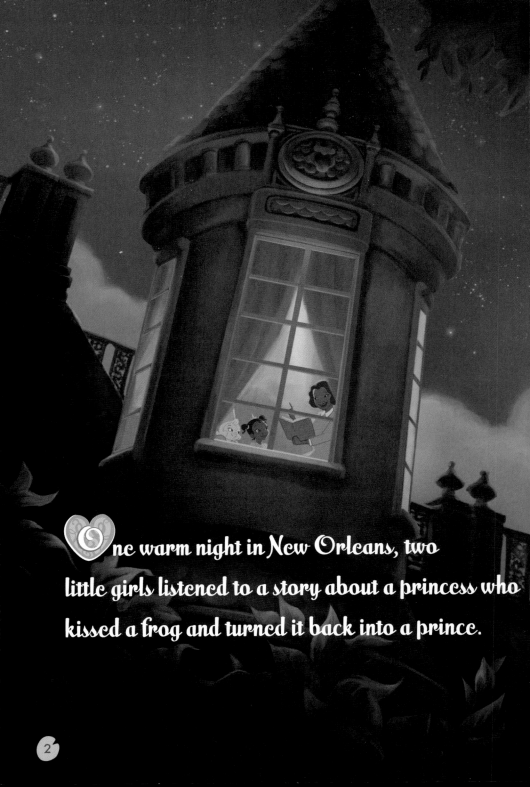

One warm night in New Orleans, two little girls listened to a story about a princess who kissed a frog and turned it back into a prince.

Little Charlotte said she would gladly *kiss* a frog to become a princess. But her friend Tiana declared, "There is no way in this whole wide world I would ever, ever, *ever*—I mean *never*—kiss a frog! Yuck!"

Tiana didn't dream about becoming a princess. Instead, she dreamed of opening up a restaurant in the old sugar mill with her daddy.

That night, Tiana wished on the *Evening Star* for her restaurant, though her daddy told her she would need to work hard to help the wish to happen. He also told her to remember what was really important: the people you love.

Tiana did work hard. When she was nineteen, she had almost enough money to buy the old mill. Sadly, her father hadn't lived to see their dream come true.

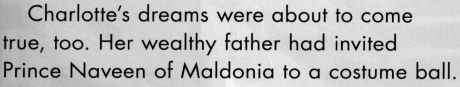

Charlotte's dreams were about to come true, too. Her wealthy father had invited Prince Naveen of Maldonia to a costume ball.

"My prince is finally coming," she cried.

Tiana agreed to bake pastries for the ball—earning the rest of the money for her restaurant.

PRINCE ARRIVES TODAY

Naveen

To Be Held

CHE
50 I
W

Prince Naveen of Maldonia
WORLDS MOST
ELIGIBLE BACHELOR

Meanwhile, Prince Naveen was enjoying
New Orleans. His grumbling servant, Lawrence,
reminded the playful prince that he needed
to marry a rich girl or find a job. After all,
Naveen's parents refused to give the prince any
more money because he was interested *only* in
having fun.

Naveen and Lawrence wound up in the company of a magician named Dr. Facilier, who used *evil magic* to cast a spell on the prince and turn him into a frog!

That night at the costume ball, Tiana was sad. The sugar mill was being sold to someone else for more money than she had. She wished again on the *Evening Star* for her restaurant, even though she didn't think it would work.

Then Tiana spotted a frog. "I suppose you want a *kiss*," she said, not expecting an answer.

But the frog replied, "Kissing would be nice, yes." Tiana screamed and ran!

The talking frog followed her, explaining that he was really Prince Naveen. If Tiana kissed him, he would turn back into a prince and help her dreams come true.

Reluctantly, she kissed him.
In a **FLASH**, things changed—but not the
way Tiana had expected. **Now *she* was
a frog, too!**

The frogs escaped from the party—and that made Dr. Facilier very unhappy. In order to carry out his plan with Naveen's servant Lawrence, the evil magician needed the real Prince Naveen.

Earlier, Facilier had given Lawrence a *magical charm* that made Lawrence look like Naveen! The fake prince attended the party to meet Charlotte, hoping to marry her. Then Lawrence and Facilier would split her fortune.

But if they didn't catch the real Naveen, the magic in the charm would run out.

Meanwhile, Tiana and Naveen had landed in the swampy bayou. Because Tiana wasn't a real princess, her kiss hadn't broken the spell.

Luckily, they met a music-loving alligator named Louis. He told them Mama Odie knew good magic and might be able to help them.

Ray, a friendly firefly, **Lit** the way to Mama Odie's place.

As they traveled, the two frogs had some eye-opening experiences and became friends.

Tiana taught
Naveen about
hard work . . .

. . . and Naveen
taught Tiana about
having fun.

When the friends met Mama Odie, she
knew what they wanted but told them they had
to figure out what they needed.

"We need to be human," Tiana explained.

"You want to be human, but you're blind to
what you *need*," answered Mama Odie.

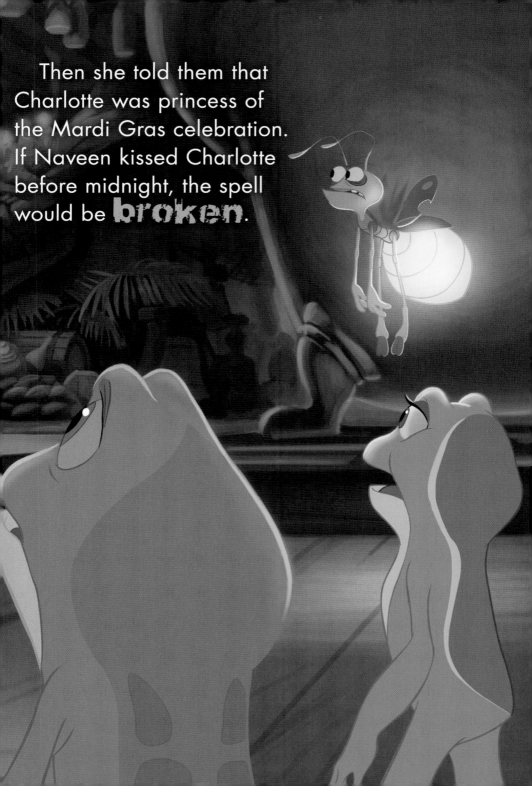

Then she told them that
Charlotte was princess of
the Mardi Gras celebration.
If Naveen kissed Charlotte
before midnight, the spell
would be **broken**.

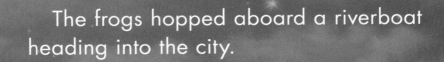
The frogs hopped aboard a riverboat heading into the city.

Naveen realized what he needed: Tiana's *love*. He wanted to marry Tiana, and he would work hard to make her dream come true.

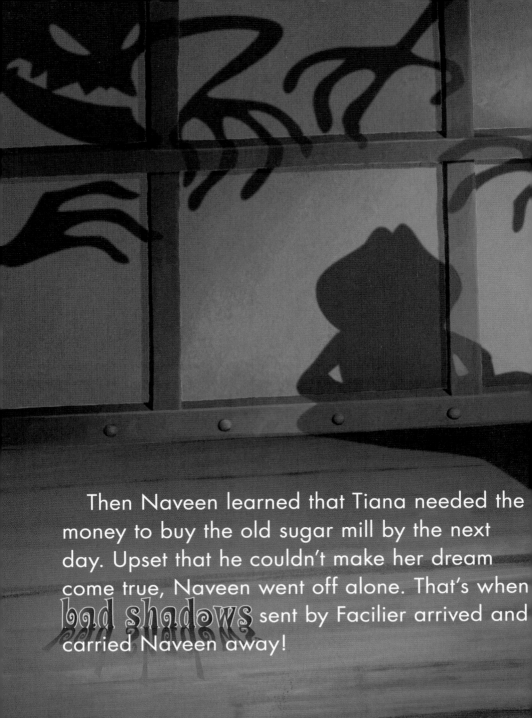

Then Naveen learned that Tiana needed the money to buy the old sugar mill by the next day. Upset that he couldn't make her dream come true, Naveen went off alone. That's when bad shadows sent by Facilier arrived and carried Naveen away!

Later, Tiana saw a human Naveen ready
to marry Charlotte. She didn't know that what
she saw was really Lawrence wearing the
magical charm, so Tiana was sad.
   But Ray knew that the *real* Naveen loved
Tiana. The firefly found the frog locked in a
box and set him free.

Naveen jumped out and interrupted the wedding.

The frog and fake prince **TUMBLED DOW**
and ended up in an empty building. Naveen
yanked the magical charm from Lawrence's
neck to end Facilier's spell.

Lawrence grabbed Naveen, but Ray
dragged the charm away. He gave the
charm to Tiana and told her what had happened.

Facilier wanted the charm and promised to give Tiana her restaurant. But Tiana recalled her father's words about what was really important: the people you love. Because Tiana loved Naveen, she  the charm! Dr. Facilier and his bad shadows disappeared forever.

The real Naveen explained everything to Charlotte, and Lawrence was arrested.

Charlotte was happy to learn that Tiana had found *true love*. She even agreed to kiss Naveen to break the spell. "No marriage required," she told the prince.

But it was too late. The clock had just struck midnight, and Charlotte was no longer a princess.

So Naveen and Tiana returned to the bayou as frogs and were married—making Tiana a real princess. This time when they kissed, *the spell was broken!*

The couple celebrated a second wedding with their human family and friends.

Working together, Tiana and Naveen soon opened Tiana's dream restaurant. They had everything they ever wanted and more important, all they would ever need: the *love* of family, friends, and each other.

Go Green

Look back in the book
with an eye that's keen:
try to spot these things
that are the color green.